What If the Rain Were Doughnuts?

by Teresa García
illustrated by Jackie Snider

Printed in the United States of America

ISBN 0-15-317307-6 – What if Rain/Doughnuts?

Ordering Options
ISBN 0-15-318653-4 (Package of 5)
ISBN 0-15-316987-7 (Grade 3 Package)

3 4 5 6 7 8 9 10 179 02 01 00

"It's still raining outside," Jessie said.

"It's more like a drizzle," said Jo.

The weather had not varied all week. The days had passed uneventfully, and Jo and Jessie were bored.

Jessie said, "We can't go outside. We can't play in the yard. I'm tired of rain!"

"I am, too," Jo said.

"What if the rain were doughnuts?"
Jessie asked.

"Hey!" Jo said. "That would be good. The
doughnuts would stack up in piles on the
fence posts."

"People would have all the breakfast they
could eat, especially if they had orange juice,"
Jessie said.

"Yes," said Jo. "We'd all be well supplied!"

"What if the rain were jokes?" asked Jo.

"Jokes?" Jessie said. "Well, people would not want to get hit by bad jokes."

"What if the jokes got damaged when they landed?" Jo asked. "Then no one would understand them. You might find only a part that said 'and then the bee laughed.' You wouldn't know what the whole joke was."

"What if the rain were banana peels?"
Jessie asked.

"People couldn't go outside," Jo said. "They
would slip and fall."

"If there were an enormous storm of them,"
Jessie said, "Homes would be damaged. People
would have to abandon them. The town would
become one big pile of banana peels!"

"What if the bananas were still inside the
peels?" Jo asked. "Then people could make a
mountain of banana bread!"

"And a river of banana milk shake!"
added Jessie.

4

"What if the rain were lemonade?" Jessie asked.

"That would be great!" Jo said. "People would run out with their juice glasses to catch it."

"I think people would get tired of lemonade after a while," Jo said. "It would be better if the kind of drink were varied."

"But soon everything would be so sticky!" Jessie said.

"What if the rain were pencils?" Jessie asked.

"Would they be sharp?" Jo asked.

"No, there'd be no point," Jessie said.

"No point?" Jo asked. Then she groaned.
"Oh, I get it! But pencils would be good. You
know how you can never find one when you need
one. When you do, it usually needs an eraser."

6

"Yes," said Jessie, "and the teacher wants us to have five sharp pencils each day. That would be all taken care of."

"There would be enough for all the schools to be supplied!" Jo said.

"What if the rain were cows?" Jo asked.

"Cows? What a funny idea!" Jessie said. "Just think. The day would begin uneventfully. Then it would start to rain. Cows would start floating down from the sky."

"I don't think I'd want more than a drizzle of cows," Jo said, looking worried.

"There would always be milk, anyway," said Jessie.

8

"What if the rain were green peas?" Jessie asked.

"Green peas? I prefer broccoli," Jo said.

"That's not the point. What if the rain were green peas?" Jessie asked.

"Everything would be green," said Jo. "We wouldn't be able to see out the windows. And I could have all the portions of pea soup I wanted!"

"You could," Jessie said. "But what if the rain were feathers?"

"I don't think I'd want portions of feathers," Jo said. They both giggled.

"Feathers would fall more like snow," Jo said. "We could use them to make feather pillows."

"I would make a feather bed!" said Jessie.

"If we fell down outside, we would never get hurt," Jo said. "The ground would be so soft!"

"What if the rain could be anything you wished for?" Jessie asked. "You could wish for clothes, or toys, or food. All of it would come falling from the sky. We could wish for all the necessities of life."

"Wishes would be the best!" Jo said. "But I'm tired of being inside. Let's go outside and play in the rain."

"Hey, Jo!" Jessie said, "Were you wishing for doughnuts just now?"

Jo laughed. "You'd better hope I don't start wishing for cows!" she said.

12

What Would You Do?

What might happen if the rain were these things?
Divide a sheet of paper in half. On one side,
write the kind of rain. On the other side, write
what might happen. (Turn the page to find
the answers.)

pencils	All the roads would be sticky but sweet.
peas	You might want to put on your slippers.
lemonade	You could write a sharp poem.
banana peels	You would need to moo-ve out of the way!
cows	You could add water and other foods and make a fine stew.

(Turn the page to find the answers.)

School-Home Connection Listen as your child reads this book aloud. Take turns with your child naming things (for example, marshmallows, flowers, birds, songs) and talking about what it would be like if they rained from the sky.

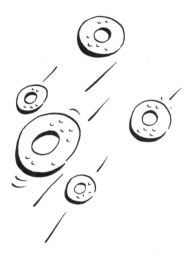

Answers:

lemonade	All the roads would be sticky but sweet.
banana peels	You might want to put on your slippers.
pencils	You could write a sharp poem.
cows	You would need to moo-ve out of the way!
peas	You could add water and other foods and make a fine stew.